Pickles & Pepper

In memory of Dorothea Lange

SIMON AND SCHUSTER BOOKS FOR YOUNG READERS
Simon & Schuster Building, Rockefeller Center, 1230 Avenue of the Americas, New York, New York 10020.
Copyright © 1990 by Donald Charles. All rights reserved including the right of reproduction in whole or in part
in any form. SIMON AND SCHUSTER BOOKS FOR YOUNG READERS is a trademark of Simon &
Schuster Inc. Manufactured in Hong Kong

10 9 8 7 6 5 4 3 2 1

Library of Congress Cataloging-in-Publication Data
Charles, Donald. Pickles & Pepper. Summary: Forced to leave their farms and search for other work, two best
friends must say goodbye until, after several years and several adventures, Pickles' music career and Pepper's
flying career bring them together again. [1. Friendship—Fiction.   2. Dogs—Fiction.]   I. Title. PZ7.C374Pi
1990   [E]—dc20   89-28202
ISBN 0-671-70345-5

Pickles & Pepper

Donald Charles

SIMON AND SCHUSTER BOOKS FOR YOUNG READERS

Published by Simon & Schuster Inc.

New York • London • Toronto • Sydney • Tokyo • Singapore

The Very Best of Friends

Pickles and Pepper lived in the Oklahoma hills. Pickles had a farm where he grew cucumbers and string beans. Just over the hill, Pepper had a farm where he grew melons and chili peppers.

Pickles and Pepper were friends. They were good friends. In fact, they were the very best of friends.

Every Saturday afternoon, they would meet at the old swimming hole for a dip. Then they would sit on the creek bank and talk until twilight.

Pickles

Pepper

"Do you remember when we were little pups how you always beat me at marbles?" asked Pickles.

"But you were better with a yo-yo," replied Pepper.

"But you beat me at miniature golf," said Pickles.

"Ah, but you learned to play the saxophone by mail order," said Pepper.

"I *do* practice a lot," agreed Pickles.

"I get all choked up when you play 'My Buddy,'" added Pepper.

"That's because we're such good friends," said Pickles.

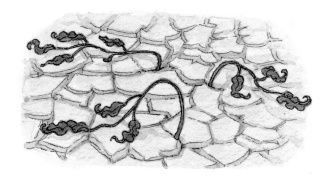

So Long, Old Pal

One summer the rain stopped falling. Day after day the sun beat down and baked the earth. The melons and cucumbers withered on the vines. The peppers and string beans shriveled and died.

Hot winds blew, and the dust towered in the sky like thunder clouds. Tumbleweeds chased one another across the bare fields.

Pickles and Pepper met in town at the ice cream parlor.

"We can't make a living on our farms anymore," said Pickles sadly. "We'll have to move on."

"I know," agreed Pepper. "Let's get aboard the next freight train and see where it takes us."

"I'm ready to go tomorrow," said Pickles.

"Let's do it!" Pepper exclaimed. "Meet me at the railroad crossing at dawn."

Very early the next morning, Pickles, with
his saxophone, waited at the railroad crossing.
Soon, he heard the mournful train whistle
in the distance, but Pepper was nowhere to
be seen.

The train huffed slowly uphill, getting ever
closer. Just as the engine began to rattle past,
Pepper appeared, running up the dusty road.

"Go ahead, climb on!" Pepper shouted to
Pickles. "I'll catch the last boxcar."

So, Pickles tossed his saxophone onto an empty flatbed car and scrambled aboard. Then, anxiously, he watched Pepper running alongside the moving train.

Just as the last boxcar rumbled by, Pepper tripped and fell. The train was going too fast for Pickles to jump off. Helplessly, he watched the small figure of his friend in the distance.

Pepper picked himself up and gazed tearfully at the vanishing train. "So long, old pal," he murmured.

Milo Hazard's Flying Circus

As the dust cleared, Pepper looked around and saw a truck stopped in the road behind him. "Want a ride?" the driver asked.

"Sure, thanks," said Pepper. "Where are you going?"

"I'm taking airplane parts back to my Flying Circus in Kansas," the driver told him.

"Any place is okay with me," said Pepper.

They drove all day and all night, trading stories.

Milo Hazard

The next morning, they arrived at an airplane hangar surrounded by cornfields. Two brightly painted biplanes stood beneath a large banner that read "Milo Hazard's Flying Circus."

After Pepper helped unload the truck, Milo
Hazard said, "Do you need a job?"

"Oh yes," Pepper replied gratefully.

"I'll teach you how to fix airplanes," Milo told
him. "I can't pay you much, but you'll get meals
and a place to sleep, and I'll show you how to fly."

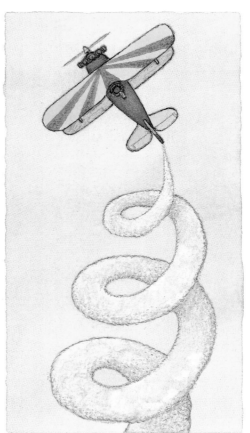

Pepper loved airplanes, and he was a quick learner. A busy year went by, and one day Milo decided it was time to leave Kansas. "We're ready to travel across the country giving rides and doing stunts at air shows," he told Pepper.

Before long, Pepper was flying a stunt plane, doing loops and spirals and nosedives to thrill the crowds. He became a star pilot with the Flying Circus.

He never forgot his friend, Pickles, though, and wherever he traveled, he looked for his old buddy.

Les Moore and the Foxtrotters

When the freight train pulled away across the Oklahoma hills, Pickles was alone and hungry. Day and night, the train rattled across hot deserts and cold mountains until it got to the orchards of California.

Pickles tumbled off, and found a job picking peaches. After the peach season he was tired, lonely, and itchy from peach fuzz.

No steady work was to be had, so Pickles picked peas and pears and plums. As he labored in the hot sun, he wondered what his friend Pepper was doing.

To ease his loneliness Pickles went to
Saturday night dances in every town he
worked. One night in Pruneville, Les Moore,
the dance band leader, went to the microphone.
"I'm looking for a saxophone player who

Les Moore

wears a size thirty-seven suit," he said. Well, Pickles wore a size thirty-seven suit, so he dusted off his old saxophone and played for the band. The very next day he was on a battered bus, touring with Les Moore and the Foxtrotters.

Every night they played a different town. Because times were hard, the band didn't attract very big crowds. Soon, Les Moore could barely afford to pay his musicians.

After a disappointing night at the Moondust Jazz Club in Hollywood, he called the band members together. "Fellows," he said sadly, "as of tomorrow, we're all out of work."

After that, poor Pickles spent his days and nights wandering the streets of Hollywood. He would put his hat on the sidewalk for donations, and play his saxophone for anyone who would listen.

My Buddy

   Meanwhile, Milo Hazard's Flying Circus had worked its way to Hollywood. When Marvin Maven, head of Monumental Movies, saw the thrilling display of barrel rolls and wing walking, he sent for Milo Hazard.

   "I'm looking for a fearless flyer to do the stunts in my new movie, *Wings Over Wyoming*," he told Milo.

   "Well," Milo said. "Pepper is my star pilot. He's the one you want."

   Pepper was delighted to work for Monumental Movies. They put him up in a big house with a swimming pool. He became a stuntman and stand-in for the movie studio's big stars.

Marvin Maven

Every day Pepper was driven to and from
the movie locations in a long limousine.
Late one night, while waiting for a traffic
light on a dark back street, Pepper heard
someone playing "My Buddy" on the
saxophone.

He knew who it was right away. He jumped out of the limousine and dashed over to the sidewalk. "Pickles!" he shouted.

"Pepper!" Pickles shouted back. They hugged each other, and drove to Pepper's big house in the hills.

"You've come upon good times," said Pickles.

"And now it's your turn," said Pepper. "I can get you a job as a studio musician, and we can be together again."

"Thank you, buddy," said Pickles. "I *did* keep my saxophone and I *did* practice."

That night, they talked while the moon floated across the sky, each one telling the other about his adventures, and recalling old times.

"What times we had!" said Pickles.

"And what times there are to come!" added Pepper.

Smiling, the two of them watched the sunrise blazing over the blue hills. They were still friends. The were still good friends. In fact, they were still the very best of friends.